MR. TOPSY-TURVY
the round way wrong

Original concept by Roger Hargreaves
Illustrated and written by Adam Hargreaves

World International

05143

If Mr Topsy-Turvy can do something the wrong way round then you can be certain that he will.

Like the way he drives a car.

Which explains why you never see him driving a car ...

... and why he travels by bus.

Mr Topsy-Turvy woke up early one morning.

He has a very topsy-turvy way of sleeping in bed as you can see.

He yawned and stretched and got up.

Then he went upstairs for breakfast.

That's right, Mr Topsy-Turvy's house is just as topsy-turvy as he is.

All his bedrooms are downstairs and his kitchen and living room are upstairs.

Mr Topsy-Turvy decided to have cornflakes for breakfast.

He opened the packet.

But being Mr Topsy-Turvy he didn't pour the cornflakes out, oh no, he poured the milk into the packet!

His meals tend to be very messy affairs.

After he had finished breakfast Mr Topsy-Turvy caught the bus into town. "One town for ticket, please," he said to the bus driver.

The bus driver scratched his head.

"Don't you mean, one ticket for town?" he said. "Right that's," said Mr Topsy-Turvy.

Mr Topsy-Turvy speaks as topsy-turvily as everything else he does.

Now, this day was a rather special day for Mr Topsy-Turvy. He had been saving up to buy a new house.

He went into Mr Homes' estate agency and said, "I'd like new to house a buy."

Mr Homes knew Mr Topsy-Turvy quite well.

"You mean, you'd like to buy a new house?"

"Right that's," said Mr Topsy-Turvy, for the second time that day.

"If you wait outside the front I'll go and get my car," said Mr Homes.

And of course Mr Topsy-Turvy waited outside the back.

After Mr Homes eventually found him they set off in the car to look at some houses.

They looked at all sorts.

Tall, skinny houses.

Short, squat houses.

Even short, skinny houses, but Mr Topsy-Turvy didn't like any of them.

None of them seemed quite right to him.

As they were driving back to town Mr Topsy-Turvy suddenly shouted to Mr Homes to stop the car.

Well, what he actually said was, "Stop car the!" but Mr Homes knew what he meant.

On the other side of a hedge was the strangest house you have ever seen.

Everything was upside-down.

In fact, everything was topsy-turvy.

And I'm sure you can guess whose house it was.

"Now, house of that's the sort want I," said Mr Topsy-Turvy.

"But ... " said Mr Homes, "But that's your house!"

"Right that's," said Mr Topsy-Turvy, for the third time that day.

"But you can't move house into your own house!" exclaimed Mr Homes. "That would be all the round way wrong ... I mean the wrong way round."

Mr Topsy-Turvy grinned a huge grin.

"Exactly," he said.

•RETURN THIS WHOLE PAGE•

3 Great Offers For Mr Men Fans

1 FREE Door Hangers and Posters

In every Mr Men and Little Miss Book like this one you will find a special token. Collect 6 and we will send you either a brilliant Mr. Men or Little Miss poster and a Mr Men or Little Miss double sided, full colour, bedroom door hanger. Apply using the coupon overleaf, enclosing six tokens and a 50p coin for your choice of two items.

Egmont World tokens can be used towards any other Egmont World / World International token scheme promotions, in early learning and story / activity books.

Posters: Tick your preferred choice of either Mr Men ☐ or Little Miss ☐

Door Hangers: Choose from: Mr. Nosey & Mr Muddle ☐, Mr Greedy & Mr Lazy ☐, Mr Tickle & Mr Grumpy ☐, Mr Slow & Mr Busy ☐, Mr Messy & Mr Quiet ☐, Mr Perfect & Mr Forgetful ☐, Little Miss Fun & Little Miss Late ☐, Little Miss Helpful & Little Miss Tidy ☐, Little Miss Busy & Little Miss Brainy ☐, Little Miss Star & Little Miss Fun ☐. (Please tick)

2 Mr Men Library Boxes

Keep your growing collection of Mr Men and Little Miss books in these superb library boxes. With an integral carrying handle and stay-closed fastener, these full colour, plastic boxes are fantastic. They are just £5.49 each including postage. Order overleaf.

3 Join The Club

To join the fantastic Mr Men & Little Miss Club, check out the page overleaf NOW!

· RETURN THIS WHOLE PAGE ·

Join Our Club!

MR. MEN & Little Miss CLUB

When you become a member of the fantastic Mr Men and Little Miss Club you'll receive a personal letter from Mr Happy and Little Miss Giggles, a club badge with your name, and a superb Welcome Pack (pictured below right).

You'll also get birthday and Christmas cards from the Mr Men and Little Misses, 2 newsletters crammed with special offers, privileges and news, and a copy of the 12 page Mr Men catalogue which includes great party ideas.

If it were on sale in the shops, the Welcome Pack alone might cost around £13. But a year's membership is just £9.99 (plus 73p postage) with a 14 day money-back guarantee if you are not delighted!

HOW TO APPLY To apply for any of these three great offers, ask an adult to complete the coupon below and send it with appropriate payment and tokens (where required) to: Mr Men Offers, PO Box 7, Manchester M19 2HD. Credit card orders for Club membership ONLY by telephone, please call: 01403 242727.

To be completed by an adult

❑ **1.** Please send a poster and door hanger as selected overleaf. I enclose six tokens and a 50p coin for post (coin not required if you are also taking up 2. or 3. below).

❑ **2.** Please send __ Mr Men Library case(s) and __ Little Miss Library case(s) at £5.49 each.

❑ **3.** Please enrol the following in the Mr Men & Little Miss Club at £10.72 (inc postage)

Fan's Name:_____Fan's Address:_____

_____Post Code:_____Date of birth:___/___/___

Your Name:_____Your Address:_____

Post Code:_____Name of parent or guardian (if not you):_____

Total amount due: £_____ (£5.49 per Library Case, £10.72 per Club membership)

❑ I enclose a cheque or postal order payable to Egmont World Limited.

❑ Please charge my MasterCard / Visa account.

Card number